Acknowledgements

I would like to acknowledge all those on my launch team for their devotion in helping gets this book on its feet.

Jon Pierce, Cit Waters, Justin Rogers, Dustin Cooper, Joe Cabral, Dustin Corvus, Shawn Connor, Courtney Mattis, Michael Lepore, Tree Fuller, Lyna (Alex), Liana Hubert, Elise Thornback, Amanda Carvajal, Jill Hernandez, Alexis (readingwithalexis), Deanna Ellison, Ava McCoy, Jennifer Dockery, Heather M, Joe Hood, Amanda (bearpiglovesbooks), Gabriel Zamora, Misha Farrel, Rosen Ravenheart, Jacob DeCoursey, Ivan Chauca, Aiden Merchant, Michael Goodwin, Paul (man_of_ideas), Becca (becsbooknook), Jess Fry, Nikki Stickney, Laurel Hasara, Tylor James, Hayley (between_history_and_horror), Adam Kennedy, Hayla Richards, Todd Young, Roxie Voorhees, Terry Pierson, Julia Lewis, Ali Ibrahim, Amy Wilson, Rebecca Lambert, Emma Tranter, Natalie Beaumont, Nick Harper, Saffron Roberts, John Mountain (Books of Blood) and my sister Debbie

Special thanks to Cecile Guillot for French translations.

First Printing: 2019

Cover Art by Elderlemon Design

ALESSA'S MELODY

A Novella

Jayson Robert Ducharme

Alessa's Melody

There is blood on my hands.

It's still warm, even though several hours have passed since they've died. I just can't bring myself to wash them. Everything stinks of iron, but that won't be a problem once I've finished with the gasoline. Henry and Frannie are in the kitchen storeroom, wrapped in tablecloths. Marshall is in his bedroom, lying in repose. And Sophie...

Sophie, ma chérie. You are with me. We are together again *never should have separated* for the first time in over half a century.

Nobody has a right to judge me. There was no malicious intent behind what happened to my baby sister *i didnt mean it please believe me* or anything else I've done. Everything I've done, I did for love. I killed for the preservation of that love—for survival itself.

Sophie... je t'aime. Please forgive me. I did this for you, and now will I die for you. *Nous mourrons ensemble.*

Alessa's Melody

February 1960
Québec

It was fifty-seven years ago, when everything fell apart.

My name is Louis Delacroix. I grew up on a farm in Le Haut-Saint-Francois, two hundred kilometers east of Montréal and not far from the American border. It was just me, Maman and Papa, and my sister Josephine. The four of us were tightly packed in a small cabin on a sprawling plain so flat it seemed you could see the edges of the world. There was a small patch of woods, telephone poles, and the occasional withering remains of a long-abandoned ranch. That was it. That was our world.

My relationship with my parents was strained. Papa and I spent the days bailing hay, feeding the chickens and horses, and maintaining our tiny three-room home. Now and then he would take me onto excursions into the countryside with our rifles to hunt for dinner. I shot and killed my first buck when I was around seven, and it was perhaps one of the few times I ever saw my father proud of me. He was a stony and distant man who worked me until I could no longer move at the end of each day. By the age of twelve I had already developed thick gray calluses on my palms and fingers.

Maman cooked and home schooled me. I remember grays in her black hair, and her face was long and sad in a wooden sort of way. Life on the farm had aged her substantially. I received plenty of affection from her growing up, but when Josephine came around, all her time was spent caring for the new baby.

Things were much different for Josephine. *Josephine.* Mon amour Sophie. I always called you Sophie, didn't I? How Maman and Papa smothered you with their love. There were times when even my father gazed down at my sister's face with a look in his eyes that I grew envious of...

I hated Sophie when she was first born. Hated that my family seemed to care only for their newly born cherub and sheltered her from the labor of the farm. Sometimes while I was outside shoveling manure in the late evening, I could see Maman and Papa in the kitchen through the window, taking turns holding and feeding Sophie.

Rejection gave me the strength to get all my work done each day, and at night I would stand over my sister's crib, coated in dirt and shivering from the miserable cold, glaring down at the small pink creature that was my baby sister. I hated her for making me feel so unwanted. I contemplated snatching her away and leaving her to freeze in the woods. Yet I held back, and I dragged myself to bed after such contemplations. I would hold on to that fire, knowing that it would keep me warm and grant me the strength to get through tomorrows woes.

When Sophie turned two, she began pining for my affection. I did my best to ignore it. During the summer she would come running out to me in the yard as I chopped wood, and she would babble at me in her baby language. Once when I returned after a hunting trip, Sophie ran up to me, flailing around a stick figure drawing she had done of me. I glared at her, paid her art no mind and stormed away. She followed me everywhere on the farm as I worked, banging sticks, trying to play me music, pulling at my clothes, and yet still I continued to ignore her.

I openly scorned her, yet she would not stop trying, and eventually her persistence wore away at my resentment. Just after her third birthday, while I was in the garden pulling vegetables, Sophie stepped outside wearing little boots and a pair of overalls. Without saying a word, she plopped down on her knees next to me and began yanking carrots out by their green hair.

I finally gave in. I moved a little closer and showed her how to properly take vegetables out of the soil without bruising them. I taught and showed her various duties all over the farm that afternoon, and she listened closely to everything I said and eagerly did what I asked.

When most everything was finished, as we walked back to the house, I asked her, "Why did you want to come out here and help me?"

Her answer came swiftly and without hesitation: "Maman and Papa don't love you like I love you, Louis."

For the first time, my heart tugged with affection for this little baby, and without any conscious volition on my part I wrapped my arms around her and told her that I loved her too.

Sophie often would sneak out of her bed in the dead of night and slip underneath my covers to cuddle with me. Whenever Papa yelled and hit me because I had done something incorrectly around the farm, Sophie would come to me when I was alone after the violence ended to hug me and share her snacks with me.

My baby sister took care of me as best as she could even when my own parents refused, and I in turn would help her with her art. She loved drawing and coloring—all the typical arts toddlers like to do. Yet, one thing she really enjoyed was music. Not just any sort of music, but specifically piano.

The only form of electronic entertainment we had in our little farmhouse was a tiny radio in the kitchen that had terrible reception. Nobody used it except for Papa, who listened to the Québec Hockey League games. One day while casually playing with the knobs on the radio, Sophie came across a classical music station and became instantly enamored by it. For hours a day, she would sit at the table with her palms resting on her cheeks and her eyes settled on the radio, listening to Bach, Chopin, and Schubert. She was fond of the *Fur Elise* in particular, and of Chopin's *Nocturnes*.

Sometimes she would stand on her chair and hold her hands in the air, pretending to perform the pieces that were playing on the radio. Maman once caught sight of her doing this and—charmed by what she was seeing—said, "Sophie, are you playing Beethoven?"

"Yep!" she said proudly.

"What, do you want to play piano when you grow up now?"

"Yep!" she said again, just as proudly. "When I grow up I'm gonna play piano and have my music on the radio too."

"Then you must devote yourself to the craft, Sophie. I think that Ferdinand or perhaps Napoleon in Chartierville have a piano you can practice on."

"Maybe I will," Sophie said. "The whole world will know who I am, and they'll play my music everywhere."

During this exchange, I was in the bathroom trying to unclog the pipes beneath the sink. I heard it all and imagined my baby sister as a famous pianist, wearing a nice suit and sitting at a grand piano, playing before an audience. It was a wonderful fantasy. Imagine that. Josephine Delacroix, the pride of the family—a famous pianist. She would have made me so proud...

Please understand. I loved my baby sister. Yes, I know I admitted that I hated her at first, and even *its my fault she* contemplated abandoning her to die as an infant, but I never did anything *hurt her yes thats* she was my everything. Ever since I lost her, the boyish young Louis Delacroix I remember being ceased to exist, and the other Louis Delacroix emerged after.

Sophie, I—

love—

February of 1960. That was when it happened. Such a cold, gloomy day it was. I was thirteen at the time, and Sophie *she was only seven.*

Maman and Papa were in Chartierville getting parts for our wood heater, which was threatening to fall apart after decades of use. Josephine and I left by ourselves, and we were instructed *so sorry maman papa we didn't think* firmly to stay indoors. They gave us a list of chores to do while they were gone—nothing demanding, just sweeping, scrubbing, and leaving the meat out to thaw.

Within a half hour we finished and were lounging around in the kitchen. I sat in a corner playing with a fold out knife, digging dirt out from under my fingernails. Sophie sat at the table listening to her piano music—specifically Brahms, I remember—and playing along in the air like she always loved to do. This was the first time in a long time that we were not under the supervision of our parents, and a sense of liberation filled us.

Sophie turned off the radio. "Let's go outside and catch a squirrel."

"How would we do that, Sophie?"

"We get a bunch of nuts and put them in a box and when one comes around we catch it."

"We should go on an adventure instead," I said, getting up. "I doubt there'll be any squirrels around. It's too cold. Let's do something we'd never be able to do with Maman and Papa around."

Sophie snatched a broom from where it had been standing against a counter and wielded it like a saber. "We could play knights!"

"Why play knights when we could have a snowball fight or build a snow castle? We can play swords anywhere."

Sophie's face lit up and she dropped the broom. "Let's do that!"

I got dressed, then helped Sophie put on her little boots and zipped up her coat. We braved the cold and went outside. The snow was so deep that I had to goose step through it, and poor Sophie had to crawl at times. I took my chère soeur by the hand to make sure I wouldn't lose her, and together we went into the woods.

A break in the trees appeared and we found ourselves standing before a massive frozen lake. I had seen this lake many times before during my hunting trips with Papa, but Sophie was seeing it for the very first time. The surface of the frozen water resembled dark green glass embroidered with twisted white frost. It was beautiful.

"Wow!" Sophie gasped. "Is this what you wanted to show me, Louis?"

"Uh-huh."

I let go of my sister's hand and leapt forward, feet firmly planting against the ice. I almost lost my balance and slipped—stupid kid that I was—but after throwing my arms out I managed to stay on my feet. Sophie stood atop the snowy bank I leapt from, looking worried.

"Come on, Sophie. There's nothing to be afraid of. I've done this before. Look." I began sliding around on the ice, my arms still out. "See? Just like hockey."

"Hockey?" Sophie said, intrigue overtaking her concern.

I turned my feet to stop myself. "Yeah, you know those games Papa listens to on the radio?"

"They do that on ice?"

"Come on, Sophie. It's fun. I'll hold your hand so you don't fall."

Carefully, like a cat approaching a bird, Sophie crept towards the ice. I took her by the knuckles, and she took a deep breath and leapt. Once on the ice, she shrieked and almost fell, but I snatched her other hand and swooped her back up to her feet. The poor girl latched onto me as if she were about to drown.

"You're okay, Sophie. I've got you."

With time, she let go of me and stood on her own. "I'm doing it, Louis!" she exclaimed, terrified and thrilled, "I'm skating!"

"You're not skating yet. Take my hand again."

I instructed her on how to move her feet. Eventually she managed to glide naturally and felt confident enough to let go of me. Laughing, she skated around, and at one point in a bout of overconfidence she tried to spin but ended up falling. "Ow!" she shouted, then started giggling. I pulled her back up and kissed her little red nose and brushed some snowflakes out of her golden hair. *Comme je t'aimais, chérie Sophie.*

At one point I found two sticks and a pinecone to teach her how to play hockey, but after an hour I decided that we should head back before our parents returned.

Sophie pouted. "I don't want to go back, Louis."

"I don't want to go back either, Sophie. But they can't find out that we snuck away. Come on."

Together we crossed the frozen lake towards land. Halfway there, sensing that Sophie was no longer with me, I stopped and looked back. She stood about seven feet behind me, halted in her tracks.

"Sophie, what are you doing?"

"Look!" she pointed.

A yard from where she stood was a half sunken tree sticking out from the ice, and upon one of its branches was perched a big white owl. Its yellow eyes were fixated on my little sister.

"It's an owl, Louis!"

"I can see that, now come on. Sophie!"

She ignored me and maneuvered towards the owl, clicking her tongue at it as if it were some sort of pet. The yellow eyes of the owl regarded her curiously from its stony white face.

"Sophie!" I barked, sliding my way towards her. "Get over here right now!"

Sophie was no more than three feet away from the owl. She held her hand out to it. "Come here, little one. I won't hurt you, petit oiseau."

Even after all this time, every exact detail—every movement and sound—still comes to my memory as if it were only yesterday. There was a loud crack, and in the next moment Sophie fell through the ice and vanished. A little squeak left her lungs, she flung her hands up, and then she was gone. The owl fluttered away as if it had been some hunter that deliberately lured its prey into a trap.

"Sophie!"

I skated to where she fell but could get no closer than a few feet from the hole in the ice. Cracks crawled towards me like deadly twisted fingers, and I knew that if I drew any nearer, the lake would swallow me as well.

I dropped to my knees and wiped snow off the ice, screaming my sister's name. I could see nothing through the pale ice save for the sickly colors of the water beneath.

One pale hand pressed itself against the other side of that frosty glass, then sank away as quickly as it had appeared, into that cold abyss.

Without reason, without warning, Sophie was gone from my life.

Alessa's Melody

December 2017
White Mountains

I turned seventy-one years old in September.

I've been a ghost since that day—a shadow of that boy. His blue eyes have grown paler, brown hair thinned out and grayed, and those rosy red cheeks have sunken in. I've lost about half of my teeth since then, my back is badly hunched, and my veiny hands have developed perpetual tremors. The boy I once was died the day Sophie drowned in that frozen lake, and this ghoul I see whenever I look in a mirror is all that remains.

It was not terribly long ago, while I was putting fresh towels in the guest bathroom cabinet, I heard a desperate voice call for me: "Louis! Help me, please!"

I rushed through the house as fast as my frail body could take me, going upstairs and into the master bedroom. Marshall was on the floor by his bed, propped up on an elbow.

"Marshall! Are you all right?"

"I just wanted to go to the fucking window," he said, pointing to the rocking chair on the other side of the room.

My heart wretched seeing him like this. Every day he got worse. Only two months ago he seemed like himself—jolly and healthy, taking bike rides and playing tennis. A mere sixty-odd days later, he became a living cadaver. Sickly pale skin pulled tightly over frail bones, heartbroken eyes peered out of his skull-like face, and his breathing was badly labored. Every day he drew closer to crossing the Styx, and his appearance was a constant reminder of that.

Swallowing my emotion, I knelt to him, feeling my weak knees crack from the endeavor. With all my strength I lifted him and walked him over to the rocking chair. He settled in, adjusted the oxygen tube on his nose comfortably, then turned his tired eyes to the window, watching the snow outside fall like white glitter.

Once I caught my breath and regained my strength, I bowed and asked, "Is there anything else I can do for you, monsieur?"

A pained look came over my old friend and master's face. "It doesn't get any easier, Del."

I knew Marshall for over half a century. All that time he was my only friend, and the only person since Sophie who treated me with any sort of love, kindness and dignity. Without him, I'd have been nothing. He had been a better father to me than my own, even though he was only seven years older than I. Seeing such a strong, beautiful man wither away like this was a miserable experience.

I placed my hand on his shoulder, and I could feel his bones through his sweaty thin skin. "I know, mon ami. I will do everything I possibly can for you."

Marshall's hand gripped mine. "You're good to me, Del. You've always been a good friend. I'm sorry you have to work yourself like this in your age for a dead bag of bones like me."

"Don't talk like that, Marshall. I wish you would hire a hospice already. I want to care for you, but I'm not a young man anymore."

Dismissively, Marshall waved his hand. "Can't afford it," he said bitterly. "Can't afford a lot of things these days if stocks keep dropping like they've been. Besides, my daughter-in-law insists on coming up here. I don't see the point, having my son get hauled away from business for my sake."

"They want to take care of you."

"My son should be focusing on what I've built. Not me."

"That can wait."

"Not in the state it is!" Marshall snapped. The sudden burst of anger exhausted him, and he took a long breath and covered his haggard face with his hand. "I've spent my whole life on

Turner Steel. And what was it all for? It's not gonna last a few months after I'm gone. It's my legacy, Del. It needs to survive."

"Your son and his family are your legacy."

Marshall quietly croaked: "I'm scared, Del."

I felt so helpless. I wish I could have told him that everything was going to be okay, but I couldn't. It would have been cruel to say such a thing.

Yet, I saw something else in him as well—a future that is soon to come to me. My days are just as numbered as his were. Two old dying men, me and him.

"Leave me, Del. I want to be alone for a while."

"Okay, Marshall. If you need anything, please let me know."

"I can't even cross a fucking room to look out a window anymore," he whimpered.

My throat tightened, and I left the room before the scene really began to affect me.

"Once he's gone, you and me are out of a job, buddy."

The kitchen was hot and chaotic that morning. Albert, the chef, had been working since about seven o' clock trying to get things ready for the arrival of Marshall's relatives. As we spoke he stood with his hands over a boiling pot, slicing potatoes into it.

I've always liked Albert, ever since he was hired here about ten years ago. He and I were the only servants left on the estate. Since stocks at Turner Steel stagnated, servants and gardeners working around the property thinned out over the years until he and I were all that remained.

"I don't think so," I told him, leaning against a counter, "Henry will be inheriting the estate after Marshall is gone. He'll need a servant and a cook."

Albert scoffed, finished cutting up the potatoes, wiped his knife against his apron and gave me a sneering look. "You really think his son is going to hold on to this old crumbing place once he's gone, in the state of the company now? Old age is making you naïve, my Canadian friend. Henry won't own this estate for more than a few months if he can sell it to keep business afloat a little while longer."

"How can you be so sure?"

"What's the point? He already has a house in Boston. It's a waste of money."

"Henry can always hire us to work in Boston, can't he?"

"I don't think so, bud. Henry has his own employees—he's not going to make any expenses on more than what he needs. Once Marshall is gone, so are we."

Hearing this made my mouth go dry. I wasn't sure what to make of it—wasn't sure if I wanted to think about it too deeply either.

"I'm not worried about it," Albert went on, grabbing a bag of vegetables from the counter. "I'm still young and everyone needs a skilled cook. I'm more worried about you, Del. You're seventy. I hate to say it but you're not as quick or strong as you used to be."

"What are you implying?"

"You know what I mean, Louis Delacroix." He looked at me seriously. "If I were you, I'd start looking for connections now, because I'm not sure what you're gonna do when the old man goes. It's gonna come soon too, if how he looks is anything to go by." He opened the bag and poured vegetables into the pot, then muttered under his breath: "Doesn't help that you're still not a citizen either."

For a long time after that conversation, I couldn't focus on anything. I tried to dust the guest bedroom and change the sheets on the beds, but I couldn't. I just stood, staring at my ghoulish self in a closet mirror, thinking. It was true. I had nowhere to go after my friend dies. Nobody will want an old, useless man when they could easily find someone young and more efficient.

The first time I met Marshall Turner was when I was twenty-two years old, during the summer of 1969. It was remarkable, because it wasn't I who initiated the friendship. Rather, it was he.

Following the death of my sister, the RCMP was only able to recover Sophie's body once the lake thawed, and she was cremated after a brief service. I was no longer welcome in my home. My mother refused to speak to me, and my father became a horrible drinker.

I was kept around strictly to continue doing work around the farm. I was ordered to labor, starving, all day outside. On the few occasions I did come in the house, my mother shamed me and my father beat me so badly that I sometimes urinated blood. No longer did I even have a bed—they segregated me to sleep in the barn among the cows and horses, no matter how cold or hot. They fed me just enough scraps for me to function, and by the time I was sixteen, I was only one hundred and ten pounds. As far as they were concerned, I was responsible for my sister's death, and they disowned me as a son. Rather, they kept me as their slave.

The discipline had become sadistic as well. If I did something wrong in my work, then Papa would lock me in the barn for days at a time, where I starved and went thirsty, exposed to the elements. I only suffered this punishment twice, but both times were so horribly traumatic that even thinking back on them now makes me violently ill. It was so cold in that barn, and after days of pure isolation, I was reduced to eating dirt and drinking either filthy horse water or my own urine. I banged against the door and screamed and pleaded to be let out. I wasn't freed either time until the fifth day.

The breaking point finally came in May of 1963. While guarding the sheep one night, rifle nestled comfortably across my lap as I lay on a pile of hay, I fell asleep by accident. When I awoke just before dawn, I found that three of our five sheep had been eviscerated by coyotes. I gazed at those ruined cadavers, their white wool coats now a dark crimson with their ribcages and entrails exposed. I knew what Papa was going to do to me as soon as he saw what I had done.

I couldn't think straight. I just stood shaking, staring at those dead sheep. I knew that I needed to do something drastic, and I had a choice between two options. One of them was killing myself—just going into the barn and shooting myself in the heart with the rifle. After mulling over this idea for several minutes, I realized that I was too cowardly to do it, and I latched onto the second option.

Sunrise appeared. The sky was no longer black, but a dark blue hue. The glimmer of the sun was orange against the flat, barren Quebecois landscape. I had to act fast.

I snuck into the house, packed a small bag with spare clothes and some canned food, then made my escape. I ran away to where I thought not even the RCMP could find me—to where nobody knew me and therefore couldn't possibly find out about what I had done to my sister. I went south and snuck across the border into New England.

It was liberating. In an unfamiliar country, I was a blank slate. No past, no relatives, no specific location I was confined to. I didn't even speak the language. I only knew about five English words—"Hello", "Goodbye", "Yes", "No", and "Beer". Other immigrants may have felt a hopeful pride upon entering this country, but I entered in a panic, convinced that border police were after me.

The first few weeks were exhausting. I camped in the woods and hunted with my father's rifle. I journeyed with the help of my compass, following signs and hitching rides from one town to another. I had a can of soup a day, which I prepared with a lighter, and went into bus stations to drink or bathe in the bathroom sinks.

The first job I landed was in Berlin, which sat along the Androscoggin River. There were many textile mills along the river, and the people running them were willing to look the other way when it came to the citizenship of their workers if it meant they could save a few dollars. It didn't matter if I was not a citizen or didn't speak English. I proved how efficient I was with my hands, and I worked for mere coins because I was desperate. There were plenty of other French workers to direct me in whatever ways I needed.

After one of the mills I was working at shut down, I gravitated towards the town of Bellevue, where I found work on the farms around the state's insane asylum Robynsville. It was here that I met another Canadian working on the hospital grounds, Gaspard Tremblay, who spoke both French and English. It was through Gaspard that I met Marshall Turner.

In the spring of 1969, after a year of working at the hospital, Gaspard told me that he found good paying work available in a nearby township called Clarke's Purchase. Some steel tycoon from Boston was building a personal estate there—a three storey mansion with a courtyard—and was looking for hard working people to build it for him. If hired, we could have our own quarters, benefits, three meals a day, and guaranteed work until the end of the year. Gaspard and I went to Clarke's Purchase immediately and were hired along with about twenty-five other people.

It so happened that the tycoon—Marshall, his name was— owned two horses and wanted them to have their own stable. Once the stable was built, I was put in charge of taking care of the horses, since I was the only one experienced with such animals. Gaspard was grouped with me since he could translate.

The day was hot—so hot that the stable was like an oven. I wore nothing but a pair of ratty jeans with the pantlegs rolled up. Gaspard was painting one of the stalls while I hammered a shoe into one of the horse's hoofs when a voice called out behind us: "Well, damn!"

A figure stood in the entrance of the stable with his hands on his hips. A Panama hat rested comfortably on his head, and he wore slacks with suspenders and a sweat stained white shirt.

"This place is coming along beautifully," the man exclaimed. He was smoking a cigar, and his face glowed orange; stern, serious, and yet playful. Neither Gaspard nor I had met Marshall Turner and didn't even know what he looked like.

"May we help you, sir?" Gaspard said.

"Just taking a gander at how things are coming along," the stranger said. Smiling at both of us, he took off his hat and began fanning himself with it. He squinted against the smoke produced by his cigar as he puffed away at it. "It's as hot as all nine circles of hell in here. I hope you boys aren't too uncomfortable."

"We're all right."

I stayed silent, focused on the horse's shoe. I didn't understand what they were saying at the time and always got shy and nervous when I was somehow involved in English conversation.

"What are your names?" the man said.

"I'm Gaspard Tremblay and this here is my friend Louis Delacroix."

I cursed Gaspard silently for getting me involved—I knew only because he mentioned my name. Nervously I turned from what I was doing, smiled awkwardly at the man—who was still grinning and fanning himself—then resumed my work.

"Those are my babies," the man said to me. "Phoenix and American Pharaoh. Them's the names they go by at the races. I've had them since they were this big"—he held his hand at his thigh. "Have you been taking good care of them? They're precious to me, my horses."

"He doesn't speak English," Gaspard said.

The man stepped over and watched me work. This was invasive and stressful. I thought he was judging me.

"They sure look healthy. Well-fed and groomed nicely." He caressed the neck of the horse, then tapped me on the shoulder and pointed at the hoof I was working on. "Mind if I look?"

Gaspard translated what he said and I stepped out of the way. The man slipped his hat back on and sat down on the stool. Gently, he lifted the horse's hoof and examined the metal shoe I had just put on. He ran his fingertips along the nail heads, went "Mmm" a few times, then nodded.

Nervously, I watched him study my work. I couldn't tell if the sweat on my face was from the heat or not.

The man placed the hoof down, pinched the cigar from his mouth, then stood. The expression on his face was unreadable. Had he found my work poor? I felt like an insect under that brazen stare.

Suddenly, he took my right hand and turned it over so that the palm faced up. Gently, he ran his thumb along the rough calluses on it. "You've got real beautiful hands, kid. These are disciplined hands... experienced hands. The only hands worth respecting." He let go and looked at Gaspard. "You said that he don't speak any English? You mind translating a few things for me and Mr. Delacroix, please?"

The conversation I had with the man follows, with Gaspard translating between us:

"Your name is Louis Delacroix, is that right? You mind if I just call you 'Del'?"

"Non, monsieur. I don't mind."

The man thumbed his hat back, produced a handkerchief from his back pocket and blotted the sweat from his forehead. "What are you good at, Del?"

"I grew up on a farm in Québec, monsieur. I know agriculture, I can take care of livestock, and I've operated all sorts of machinery and farm equipment. I've also cooked and maintained our house, including the plumbing and electricity."

"You're a good worker, Del. Wanna know how I know? Because I've had dozens of Boston yuppies take care of my babies here, and no matter how many times I show them, they can never get a single god damned horseshoe on straight. You did a fabulous job."

"Merci, monsieur."

"You got a permanent place of employment? A place to live?"

I hesitated to answer, then decided to be honest. In the face of the man before me, I felt like he wouldn't cast me aside like so many others had. "I'm not a legal citizen. I came to the United States illegally. I have no home."

For a long time he considered me, puffing his cigar and rubbing his rough, unshaven chin with the ball of his thumb. Finally, he took the cigar from his mouth, put it out against the heel of his leather shoe, then spat. "If I give you a place to stay and some cash in your pocket, would you meet with a tutor to learn some English so that you could work for me?"

My heart leapt into my throat. I couldn't believe what I was hearing. "Yes, absolutely!"

"Stick around after the estate's done. I'm Marshall Turner, of Turner Steel."

That is how I met my best and only friend.

After finishing my remaining duties, I decided to check on Marshall. When I stepped in and saw him unmoving in his chair with his eyes closed, my heart rose into my throat. I rushed over to him and put my hand on his shoulder. "Marshall!"

His eyes opened. "Huh?"

Relief washed over me. "I… wanted to see how you were feeling, monsieur."

"Better," he managed, "not amazing, but my head is better. Could you help me back to my bed?"

Taking him by the arm, I walked him to his bed and lay him down in it, then adjusted his sheets and made sure the tube to his oxygen was on properly.

"I'm sorry, Del. For earlier."

"It's nothing, Marshall."

"Is everything ready?"

"Yes. Your son and his family will be here by two o' clock tomorrow. Albert is already preparing dinner for this evening and for tomorrow."

"I'm nervous, Del. I haven't seen my son in person for five years. I've called him for the holidays, sure, but I can't help but feel like I've been estranged from his family for too long."

"They're coming to stay with you because they care about you, Marshall."

"I feel like I've been a bad grandparent."

"Your family will be happy to see you. You'll see."

"You sure?"

"Absolutely."

Marshall's eyebrows went flat. "Say Del, you've never actually met my granddaughter yet, have you?"

"Only once, monsieur. I met her that one time your family came up here for Christmas perhaps seven years ago. I believe she may have been only a year old at the time."

"Ah. Well, she's pretty grown up by now."

"I'm sure."

"She's a gift, according to my son. Bright, quick witted, talented. You know she plays music?"

"Really?" My interest suddenly piqued. "What instrument?"

Marshall smiled. "Piano. She's become quite the pianist. I've heard her play over the phone a few times. It's amazing really, for an eight-year-old girl."

I smiled, but it was a forced smile. It was only natural for me to hear this and think of Sophie. "That's good, monsieur. Perhaps she'll play on the piano for you in the lounge?"

Marshall managed a grin. "I'm tired, Del."

"You must take your medications before you go to sleep."

A groan left him. "Fine." He turned his head and muttered: "Shit tastes like expired milk."

I gathered his medicine from the cabinet and helped him take them. For several minutes afterwards I stayed with him until he fell asleep. It seemed like the only time he was ever at peace anymore was when he was asleep. I closed his curtains and stepped out, then went downstairs into the cellar where my quarters were.

It's a decent room, despite its location. I have everything I need here—bed, lights, bookcase, desk, heat. It's always been my quiet place to be alone—to think. I kept myself busy each day to keep my thoughts away, so whenever I retired to my dark quarters, it was when I was at my most intimate with my soul.

I feel that I have little control over my thoughts and emotions. They have a will of their own. It tortures me. They carry me to terrible places and make me feel terrible things. Sometimes they make me gaze at the laces of my spare shoes or go upstairs and consider the shotgun hanging over the fireplace in the lounge. I think about when I awoke to those eviscerated sheep all those years ago, and how I could have ended it all right there.

I've lived longer than I thought I would. Youth is gone. I'm withered, slow, and my mind has gone significantly. Life is almost over. It's not death itself that frightens me—it's that I don't know when it will come. When I least expect it, my heart could seize, or an aneurism could strike me, or a cell inside my body could mutate and grow out of control.

Out of everything though, dying in my sleep scares me worst of all. I don't like the idea of falling asleep and not waking up. I want to be aware—as horrible as it may be—of what's happening to me. I want to be prepared to die, knowledgeable of it. I know that sounds strange. What I'm trying to say is that I want to feel ready. I want to leave this world when I feel like I haven't left anything unfinished, or when it doesn't seem so scary.

With suicide, you can prepare. You can finish what you must, say what you need, and when you're ready you can go. It's up to you how peaceful it can be. By taking my own life, I am denying the fates any power over me. I don't have to wait, like Marshall, dwelling on all my regrets in my final moments. Suicide… makes me feel safe. Suicide is control over one's own fate.

Yet, I'm still terrified of dying.

I have always wanted to die, but I'm too scared to. That's what keeps me from going through with it. I don't know what lies beyond—can't even fathom. I have no religious beliefs to bring me comfort with my own mortality. Yet, I know I must face my fears soon, because I don't have much time left, and *I must be in control!*

There are two primary reasons why I desire death. One comes from the fact that I have wasted my life. I'm seventy years old, and I know that I have done nothing worth remembering. I've never had a romantic partner, children, or achieved any great accomplishment. When I die, there will be no evidence that I existed. I can't think of anything more horrible than that. It's too late now to try anything, and it makes me want to drift away from existence altogether so I can be spared this despairing fact.

The second reason is Sophie.

It's been fifty-seven years since that awful day in Canada. Maman and Papa always reminded me, with every beating and every shame, that it was my fault. I murdered my sister. Those days when Papa would beat me senseless, he would shout "Murderer!" until I broke—made me believe that I deserved it. I did deserve it. I should be thankful they didn't turn me over to the RCMP.

Sophie was my single and most powerful experience with love. To be responsible for her death is something that has haunted me my entire life. This is the primary reason why I wish to die. Besides my parents, I have never told a soul about how my sister died. Not even Marshall knows.

Every day, I have thought about that day, feeling the same crushing and inconsolable grief eating away at me like cancer. I want to be freed from this filthy secret, yet nobody can know. I wouldn't last a minute in prison at this age. They would devour me alive.

When my thoughts turn to Sophie, I often go to my desk and dig out the only two remaining things I have of her existence—a photograph and a necklace with a key on it. Papa took the photograph and I made the necklace for Sophie myself with an old iron key.

The photo is discolored from age and corroded from the oils of my fingertips. It was taken perhaps in the summer of 1958. Sophie and I are in front of the farmhouse, and I am holding Sophie from behind, my face pressed against the side of hers, and we are both smiling brightly.

Sometimes I stare at this photograph and hold the key of the necklace close to my heart for hours. I wish I could run my fingers through her hair again. I want to smell her, kiss her, and cuddle her late in the night.

I'll give my life to you someday, Sophie. It is everything I have to give—my measly, worthless life. For you, mon bébé, mon trésor, ma moitié. No matter how many years have passed, I will always love you.

Je mourrai pour toi, mon bébé,

On the afternoon of December 18th, Henry and Francine Turner, along with their daughter Alessa, arrived at the estate after a three-hour drive from Boston.

Marshall was in his wheelchair by a window in the living room, watching the front gate, waiting. I asked him several times if he needed anything, but each time he declined, never taking his eyes away from the window.

I understood how he felt. Years ago, Marshall used to go down to Boston to visit his son and his family every holiday. After he retired and handed his position of CEO to Henry however, he stopped going down at all, and instead would send cards or make phone calls on special occasions. The trip down, in Marshall's words, was too exhausting for him at his age. It was sad, to see how far Marshall and his son had drifted. I imagine some part of him felt ashamed to see his estranged family again during his time of need.

I was anxious as well. I helped raise Henry when he was growing up on the estate. I changed him as a baby, fed him, helped him with his schooling lessons, and even taught him to ride a bicycle. After he graduated from Suffolk and got married,

Henry settled in Boston and I saw him less and less. It was a little sad for me, because I had grown attached to him—it was like having a sibling again.

The last time I saw Henry or his family was seven years ago, during Christmas of 2010. He and Francine came up and brought Alessa with them, who was only a year old at the time. Even as a baby, the girl was quiet and reserved. I wondered what she would be like now.

At 12:30 Marshall called for me, his voice frail: "Del! They're here!"

I rushed to the living room. Marshall was clutching his bony chest and trying to clear his throat. I patted him on the back. "Monsieur, you shouldn't strain yourself yelling like that."

"Look," he croaked, pointing.

Through the window I saw a dark blue BMW passing through the front gates of the estate.

"Bring me downstairs, Del. We have to greet them. I want to see my son again. I want to see my granddaughter."

I wheeled him outside and onto the front porch. Henry Turner stood next to his car with his arm resting neatly on the roof. He had changed little in the time since I last saw him— some wrinkles around his mouth and grays in his hair around the ears. He wore sunglasses and smiled as I wheeled his father out.

"Hey, dad," he said.

"Hey, kid."

Henry stepped onto the porch and gave his father a hug. "It's good to see you again."

Marshall scoffed. "Get the hell outta here. Where's Frannie?"

As if on cue, a dark-haired woman wearing a scarf and black dress lumbered out of the BMW with a huge bouquet of flowers. "Merry Christmas, Marshall!" she exclaimed, stepping onto the porch.

Marshall took the flowers and pressed them against his chest. "Good Lord, what's with all the sentimentality?" he said, his voice cracking. "Frannie, you've always been a sweetheart. Come here."

They hugged, and all three began to talk casually. Frannie and Henry were tactful, made no mention of Marshall's appearance and instead talked about the weather, business and life in Boston. Marshall's anxieties seemed to vanish—he stopped shaking and fiddling with his oxygen tube.

As Frannie and Marshall chatted, Henry stepped up to me. "Del," he said.

"Monsieur." I bowed and we shook hands.

"It's good to see you're still around, Del."

"For better or worse, mon ami."

"Did you get my card?"

Henry had sent cards to both me and his father for Thanksgiving. "Yes, I did. Thank you very much."

Henry peeked over his shoulder at his wife and father, who were still talking, then lifted his sunglasses so that they rested on top of his head. With the glasses off, I could see in his eyes the devastation he felt at the sight of his father. "How is he, Del? I didn't want to say anything, but he looks so much worse than I imagined."

I swallowed. "Not well. I've been caring for him as best as I can, but yesterday he collapsed. I had to carry him across the room. He's in a lot of discomfort."

Henry's eyes glassed over and he looked away. "How much longer do you think he has?"

"I don't know, monsieur. I'm sorry. I'm not in any position to say, and I don't wish to get your hopes up."

"God damn it, dad. Why couldn't you have told us sooner?" He pulled his sunglasses back down. "Del, listen. You're a good guy. More than just an estate servant. You took care of me when I was a kid and you've gone above and beyond taking care of my dad. I can't tell you how much this means to me, and I wish I could have come up sooner."

"All this is very sudden, mon ami. Marshall put off seeing a doctor for a very long time. When he finally did, he didn't tell anyone until several weeks after he was diagnosed. Nobody was prepared. Do not blame yourself."

"Henry!" Marshall said. "You and Del keeping secrets from me?"

Henry cleared his throat and turned to his father. "Nah, pops. Del and I were just catching up. He brought up that time I busted your fish tank when I was eight years old."

"You still owe me for that, you little rat," Marshall said. "You were such an uncontrollable little hellion. I'm sure Del can contest to that. Can't you, Del?"

"Absolutely."

"Where's my granddaughter anyway? I haven't seen her since she was a baby. I want to see how big she's gotten."

"She's in the car," Frannie said. "Sorry, I'll go fetch her. She was nervous about coming up and didn't sleep well last night, so she ended up napping in the backseat on the way up."

Frannie returned to the car and opened one of the rear doors. Alessa hopped out. As soon as I saw her, the blood drained from my face.

"Alessa, sweetheart!" Marshall called. "Come see your grandpa!"

The little girl had golden hair and wore a dark green coat with a beret. She trotted onto the porch with her hands laced bashfully behind her. "Hi grandpa," she said.

Marshall ran his fingers through her hair—her beautiful, familiar hair—and he admired her peachy, soft face. "It's so good to see you again, girl. Last I saw you, you were"—he held his hands before him in measurement—"this big. You were tiny, you know that? And look at you now!"

Alessa's cheeks blushed. "Thanks."

"You still playing piano? You'd better not stop or I'll have to whup your butt."

"She can already play Schubert and Chopin pretty well," Frannie said. "She's gotten real good at *Nocturnes.*"

"Is that so?" Marshall looked at his granddaughter with obvious pride. "You're a music prodigy, kiddo. Don't ever stop. Would you play me some piano later this evening in the lounge?"

"Of course, grandpa."

"Good kid."

The family chatted and caught up, but I don't remember any details of what they talked about. It was as if my entire world had shattered like glass, and the only thing left was that little girl. Sweat soaked my clothes, my knees trembled, and my mouth went dry.

The little girl looked exactly like my dead sister Sophie.

"Del?" Henry said. "You all right? You're looking a bit pale."

I tried my best to regain my composure. "Yes," I said faintly, "I think I'm just tired. It's been a terribly long few weeks."

Without warning, the little girl—*her*—crept up to me and squinted at me curiously. Terror overcame me, and I couldn't look at her.

"What's your name?" she asked.

I swallowed, smiled, and forced myself to look at her. "Louis Delacroix, mademoiselle."

"Are you a butler?"

"Of sorts."

"Are you from France?"

Henry pulled her away gently, laughing with a hint of embarrassment. "Canada, sweetheart. He's from French Canada. Forgive my daughter, Del. She's a curious one."

"Of course." I secretly thanked him for getting her away from me. My instincts screamed at me to stay away from her. If she touched me in that moment—good Christ, I think I would have screamed.

"Let's go inside," Marshall said, turning himself to the door, "it's damned cold out here."

Throughout dinner I had to fight with myself to keep from looking at her. It was like avoiding Medusa. Once I seated and served everyone, I crept into the corridor and gazed into the dining room, staring at her. The resemblance was uncanny—the eyes, nose, mouth, even how tall she was and the pitch of her voice. She was only a year older than Sophie was when she passed away, and loved to play piano like Sophie dreamed of doing.

I kept telling myself that it couldn't be. All of it must have just been a coincidence. Yet my heart screamed otherwise. Logic and emotion clashed; I felt as if I had lost control of both.

After dinner we stepped into the lounge, where Marshall's old piano was. We all sat and watched Alessa perform, her tiny hands effortlessly searching for each precise key without a mistake.

To see before my eyes such talent in a young girl was remarkable. Effortlessly, Alessa played Chopin's Prelude in F Sharp Major and *Clair de Lune* and Bach's *Goldberg Variations*—all favorites of Sophie. My hands knitted tightly together, enamored and frightened by this little girl.

"She's got Chopin down pat. She's good with slower pieces right now," Henry said, "the faster ones are a bit trickier for her."

"For her birthday we're bringing her to a George Winston concert—he's playing in Boston." Frannie said.

"When's her birthday?" I asked.

"April 7th."

That cold terror was aggravated further. Sophie was also born in April, though on the 22nd, not the 7th. Still, it couldn't have been a coincidence. It was as if she never really ceased to exist at all.

"Over the summer we're having her audition to play in a live concert with professionals," Frannie said, "we're so proud of Alessa. She's such an angel."

"Yes," I said. "An angel."

Alessa finished, turned in her chair and gave a subtle bow. Everyone applauded her. "Beautiful, just beautiful," Marshall said. "We're proud of you, girl. I can't believe I waited until now to hear you play in person."

After a long evening, I showed the Turners to the guest room, where their beds were prepared. Alessa hopped on her bed and kicked her legs off the edge as if she were on a swing.

"You look sick, Del. You've been sweaty and pale all day," Henry said as he unpacked his suitcase.

"It's just the stress of it all, monsieur Henry. Taking care of Marshall has been exhausting and emotional."

"Of course, Del. You're not young either, you know. It's a lot of work to care for somebody else. I can't imagine how tired you are."

"But now you can rest," Frannie said. "We'll look after Marshall from here on out."

"Yes," I said. "I'll go lay down now."

"Thank you, Louis," Alessa said. She was smiling at me—a smile I recognized. A bead of sweat rolled down my temple.

"Bonne journée," I said to the Turners, then dismissed myself before I completely fell apart. As soon as I went down to the cellar and entered my quarters, I began to sob hysterically.

For hours, I couldn't calm down. I paced my quarters as my thoughts raced and tormented me. I fell into crying fits intertwined with bouts of anxiety and confusion.

It had to be a coincidence. I kept telling myself that, yet I couldn't believe it. The passion for piano, the birth month, the similar features and the voice? The very same pieces Alessa played happened to be some of Sophie's favorites. No way it could have been mere coincidence.

I took the photograph of Sophie out of my desk and stared at it, examining details I had mulled over countless times before, trying to compare her appearance to that of Alessa.

If Alessa really was a second coming of Sophie, then why? After so long? After what I did to her? Had the fates taken pity on me, knowing that I've suffered for so long and am soon to die?

Perhaps I was being given a second chance—an opportunity to redeem myself before my death. It was the only thing that made sense to me. Yet how could I redeem myself in the presence of Sophie's return? I didn't even know if all this was really true or a product of my own hysteria. They were all just ideas—ideas I wanted so desperately to be true.

The only way I could know the truth was to become close to Alessa. I would have to take very good care of her and pay close attention. There was a chance that I could have been wrong, but I had no idea how to prove it. I just needed to be observant, patient, and wait...

In the morning, after troubled sleep, I found Frannie and Alessa in the lounge. Alessa was playing Tchaikovsky pieces on the piano while Frannie unpacked a big box of red, white and green ornaments.

"Good morning, Del," Frannie said. "You look tired."

"I am tired," I said, rubbing my face. "I did not sleep well. What have you here, mademoiselle?"

"Can you believe it? Marshall hasn't put up a Christmas tree in this big miserable house in years. He told me so just last night."

"I never needed to because I stopped having people up here for the holidays," Marshall called, wheeling himself into the room. "You're wasting your time, Frannie. I'm probably not even gonna to make it to Christmas."

"All the more reason to make things around here a bit merrier," Frannie said, lifting a glittery snowflake ornament from the box. "That's what Christmas is all about, Marshall. Love and being with family. That's just what you need."

"A new cancer-free pancreas off the black market would be a bit better."

"Excuse me?"

"Nothing." Marshall rolled his eyes. "What do you think, Del? Is all this horseshit or is Christmas really about love and family?"

I bit my lip and regarded Alessa, who sat at the piano with her back facing us, engaged in her playing. "Yes," I said. "I think it is. Where is Henry?"

"He's out getting the tree," Frannie said. "He'll be back in a few hours."

Tactfully, I cleared my throat. "Excusez-moi, but breakfast will be served shortly."

"Fantastic!" Frannie snapped her fingers. "Alessa, could you come over here and help me with the rest of these?"

Alessa ceased her playing, hopped off the stool and went to her mother. Together they unpacked the rest of the ornaments.

After breakfast, Henry returned wearing a heavy coat and gloves, lugging a small tree under his arm. His face was bright red from the cold and snowflakes fell from his hair. He set the tree down in a makeshift stand in the lounge, then he, Frannie and Alessa spent the afternoon decorating it. Alessa went around the tree with tinsel and Frannie set a glowing angel figure on the top. When it was finished, Alessa stepped back and admired the tree, her face beaming with pride.

"Alessa, wake up your grandfather," Frannie said.

During the decorating Marshall had dozed off in a corner of the room. Alessa shook him awake, and he came to dreamily and saw the tree. His eyes widened in excitement at the sight of the angel on top, but then relaxed. "Oh," he muttered. "I'm still alive."

"What do you think?" Frannie said. "Merry Christmas!"

"Yeah, it's uh"—he began lifelessly, but upon seeing his granddaughter's pleading eyes, he softened his attitude—"it's beautiful. Absolutely beautiful. Thank you for this."

The Turners gathered around the tree together. I watched them from afar, through a crack in the doorway as I stood out in the hall. My heart wrenched. I wished so badly to have what the Turner family had. My boyhood Christmases were always so cold and unhappy.

Mostly though, I wished to be close to Alessa.

For the next few days, I observed Alessa's every movement and listened to every sound she made. All of it left me feeling convinced that she was, indeed, my sister returned. The more convinced I became, the stronger my feelings for Alessa grew. I had so much I felt I needed to say to and ask her, many things I yearned to share with her—all of it was just building up inside me.

Yet, I just had no definite proof. How was I going to prove it? It had to be subtle enough so that my suspicions weren't obvious, but clear enough for me know for sure.

The opportunity came on the fourth night of the Turners' stay at the estate. Sometime around midnight, as I sat at my desk clutching my photograph of Sophie, the wineglass droplet sounds of piano strings was heard. I didn't notice it at first, as my thoughts were so intense, but in a moment of clarity the music came to me. I didn't recognize the piece being played, but it was beautiful.

It must be Alessa playing, I thought. Yet why at such an hour?

The piano strings wove themselves together in an elegant and seductive piece. It drew me in, and I closed my eyes and let the music take me away. Alessa was trying to get my attention. Why else would she be playing so late at night? It was because she knew—knew who I was and who she was. This was her way of expressing it to me, because like me she was afraid of what her family would think.

An idea came to me. I took Sophie's key necklace from my desk, put it in my pocket and crept out of my dark quarters. Down the corridor leading to the lounge, the piano notes drew me towards her like a moth to the flame. I stood before the lounge door—I didn't want to go in just yet. I just stood and listened, taking the music in.

Alessa finished her piece and then... silence. My eyes opened and I felt my heart struggle. Why did she stop? Swallowing, I opened the door an inch so that not so much as a squeak in the hinge could be heard, then peeked in.

In the darkness, Alessa sat hunched over the piano keys wearing her nightgown, unaware of my presence. I opened the door the rest of the way, allowing light from the corridor into the room. It was then did she finally notice me. She squinted at me like some cat in the dark, trying to figure out who had found her.

"Mademoiselle Alessa?" I said, stepping in. "It's late."

"Louis? The butler?"

"Are you okay?"

"I'm okay, I guess."

"You only guess."

Alessa bit her lip and turned on her bench to better face me. "Am I in trouble?"

"What? Trouble? Goodness, no. Not in the slightest, madame. I just"—I considered my next few words carefully—"was drawn. To your playing."

Alessa's face relaxed. "You were?"

"Yes. It was just beautiful music. I didn't recognize it, though. What was it that you were playing?"

She shrugged. "Just something I came up with."

"You wrote such music?"

"Well, I didn't write it." She smiled meekly and tapped her finger against her temple.

"Surely you're kidding."

"Nope."

"How many pieces have you memorized? That you've come up with yourself?"

"A few. I come up with my own music all the time." She gently pressed down on a key, allowing the string to vibrate in the body of the piano until it went dead. "Sometimes when I'm home alone I sit at my piano all day and play. I just tap random keys and listen to what sounds good, and I keep going until I have a whole composition. Late at night, when my parents are asleep, I play the stuff I made by myself."

"That's incredible," I said. "But why play your own pieces in secrecy? Do your parents not recognize your talent?"

"They do. But I don't want to play my own pieces for them. I play them for myself. I wish they didn't see any talent in me."

"How could you say such a thing? You are a prodigy. Your talent will bring you so much in the future."

"I feel like that's all I am. I'm lonely."

"Why?"

"I hate living in Boston. I hate that my mom and dad make me spend all day at the piano. They make me learn all these pieces I don't want to learn, making me go to these stupid concerts where everyone is old and boring. They even have a tutor teach me school lessons at home. I love to play piano, but I love playing it for me. I want to have friends instead of practicing all the time and doing everything my parents want me to do."

"Have you spoken to them about this?"

"My dad just says that one day I'll thank him. He told me that when he was growing up, grandpa Marshall raised him the same way—had him home schooled so he could learn business. He says that America is full of competition, and the earlier you start getting good at what you want to do, the better chance you have of being 'ahead of the curb'—that's what my dad calls it.

That's what grandpa always told him and that's what my dad always tells me. But I don't care."

Seeing her like this—this beautiful child—made me want to take her in my arms and hold her tightly. I wanted to take her loneliness away, but I had to resist. My affection for Alessa grew significantly listening to this young, articulate girl speak.

"A movie was on TV a few days ago," she went on. "In it all these kids went to a summer camp together. They swam in a lake and played music around a campfire, laughing and having fun." Her eyes began to glass. "I wish I could have that. I wish I had friends who cared about me."

I knelt to be eye-level with her. "I too understand this pain. I grew up on a farm in Québec. My parents did not love me. At least, I don't think they did. I did nothing but work my whole childhood. Look."

I held my withered hands to her, so that she could see the blackened thick skin on my fingers and palms from the years of labor I endured. Alessa seemed fascinated by them.

"I began working around the farm when I was six years old. I grew up knowing no love, and I had no friends."

Alessa's brow went up in sympathy. "I'm sorry, Louis."

My opportunity came. I needed to observe how she reacted; even the slightest expression or gesture could be an indication that she knew, or that there was something deep down inside her that she recognized.

"The only person I had in my life was my baby sister, Josephine. I always called her Sophie. She was the love of my life—the only person that gave me strength during those difficult years."

"Where is she now?"

"She's gone."

I watched Alessa's face. The only expression she gave was shock. It wasn't enough.

I went on: "When I was thirteen, she drowned in a lake after falling through ice."

Alessa shook her head at me. I sensed no recollection in her, no buried memories suddenly emerging. "I'm so sorry to hear that, Louis," she said. "It's amazing, what you've survived in life. You're a very strong man."

"Thank you," I said. Despite the disappointment I felt at her not remembering what happened to her, I felt tender when she said this to me. I refused to give up. Perhaps what I told her just wasn't enough to make her realize yet. I had to do more to help stir her memory.

"You should go to bed, mademoiselle," I said. "It's very late."

"It is. Thank you for admiring my music, and for listening to me, Louis."

"Absolument, ma précieuse amie." Anxiety rose within me—that same feeling you may perhaps get when asking a girl out on a date. "Listen, I'd like you to have something."

"What?"

I dug from my pocket the key necklace. "I'd like you to have this. It was once my sister's. If you ever need a friend, please talk to me. I will be more than happy to keep you company and serve you."

"Geez, Louis… this is really sweet, but are you sure you want me to have this? It feels wrong, to take something that belonged to your sister."

"It is yours. I do not have much time left in this world. I feel that it is better if I gave you something of my sister to carry on after I'm gone. Take it. And please, wear it whenever you can."

I put the necklace in Alessa's palm and she squeezed it. "Thank you, Louis."

"Of course."

"You know, my dad really admires you. He always talks about you, says that you're more than just a butler. You're a good friend who really cares. I can see what he means."

I was so touched that I wanted to weep, but I kept my composure. "Thank you. Run along to bed now. Go, before your parents figure out your late-night excursions. And Alessa?"

"Yes?"

"Don't stop playing late at night." I paused, feeling intimidated by my sudden request. "I have trouble sleeping at night, you see. I think a lot… too much, in fact. Your music makes me feel okay. It takes my bad thoughts away and relaxes me. Would you keep playing for me?"

"Of course, Louis," Alessa said, smiling. "I'll play just for you."

I swallowed my emotion and cleared my throat. "Thank you, Alessa. Your music is like a lullaby to me."

Together we stepped out of the lounge and went our separate ways in the corridor. Once returned to my quarters, I felt refreshed, like I was fifty years younger. It was amazing. My precious sister—my baby. For the first time in fifty-seven years I shared an intimate moment with my sister. I cried in joy, then lay in my bed, fantasizing.

That necklace will stir memories and sensations in her, I told myself. She'll realize who she is in due time. Alessa will be Sophie again. We will be together again.

Nous serons ensemble à nouveau.

The following morning Albert made breakfast and left me with a platter to serve everyone with. We chatted for a bit, then I went to the dining room where everyone was sitting around the table talking. The family greeted me warmly, Alessa included, who smiled brightly and waved.

"Morning, Del," Henry said. "How are you today?"

"Delightful, mon ami."

I served Henry and Frannie first, then went to where Marshall sat at the head of the table. My friend was not looking well. His eyes were half open, seeming far away somewhere in his head. When I set his plate before him I nudged him gently and told him it was nice to see him, to which he seemed to awaken from his trance and smiled at me.

Lastly I served Alessa her plate of benedict and toast, grinning pleasantly, happy to see her again. However, when I got close enough, I saw something that immediately sapped me of any joy. Instead an ugly boil formed in my stomach.

She was not wearing her necklace.

I set the plate down before her and swallowed my offense. "How are you this morning, madame?" I managed.

"Great, Louis," she said. "How are you?"

I forced a smile and hid my hands behind my back so that she could not see them trembling. "Very good," I said. I wanted to pull her aside and ask why she wasn't wearing her necklace—

something that was of utmost importance to her character, but I refrained. Perhaps she was going to put it on later in the day. This thought calmed me—for the time being.

Yet, Sophie's necklace appeared nowhere for the rest of the day. Alessa played piano, went outside with her mother in the snow, chatted with Marshall for several hours, but at no point did she ever put on the necklace.

Once my duties were finished I returned to my quarters enraged. I paced my room, grabbing what little hair remained on my head, cursing the air as if I were cursing at Alessa. A dagger had been pierced through my soul. How could she do this? Does she not realize who she is?

Another offense came late in the night. After waiting anxiously for hours, I did not hear Alessa playing piano upstairs in the lounge. Midnight passed, then one o'clock. The silence throughout the estate was crushing. Why wasn't she playing? She said she would play just for me! Did she want to hurt me? I couldn't think of any other reason why she wouldn't play.

No longer did I tolerate waiting. I went upstairs and into the empty lounge. The cover over the piano keys was undisturbed. I lifted the cover and let my finger glide along the keys without pushing any down.

Like a thief in the dark I crept through the estate and entered the guestroom. The shapes of the three Turners were visible beneath their sheets. Two in the queen bed, and a smaller shape in the guest bed. Upon seeing that small shape, the greatest affection fluttered through my stomach and searing rage filled my heart.

The bureau for Alessa's things stood near her bed. I quietly opened the drawers and dug through her dresses, shirts and underwear. In one of the top drawers I found it—Sophie's key necklace. Like some piece of trash, Alessa had discarded and forgotten it among her laundry. I clutched the necklace in my fist, feeling my body go cold.

I went to Alessa's bed and stood over her. Her beautiful face, partially hidden by her hair, did not stir at my presence. My hand unconsciously rose and held itself over her head. I wanted to grab her by the hair and—

No, I thought. I can't allow myself. It was simple—the necklace just wasn't enough to stir the girl's memory of her previous life.

My anger soothed and I began to calculate. No way could I allow her to repress her reawakening any further. I would have to do something else to make her realize who she was, and do it in such a way that she wouldn't have any choice but to accept it. Forward and direct, so that it couldn't be discarded and forgotten about in some drawer.

I knew exactly what to do.

My violent emotions simmered and instead I felt only intense love for Alessa. Gently, I placed the key of the necklace into the little girl's open palm, closed her fingers around it, and kissed her gently on the temple. "Je t'aime, chère sœur," I whispered. The girl winced, but then went still.

I stepped out of the guest room and closed the door. *I made you mine again baby Sophie yes for us I did it for us.* Everything was going to make sense soon.

I slept for only four hours before I had to begin my morning duties. Albert was in the kitchen, preparing breakfast for the Turners per usual. We greeted each other, then I took the platter of food he had prepared. Just as I was about to step out, he stopped me.

"Louis, just a moment."

I stopped in the doorway and turned to him. "Yes, Albert?"

He cleared his throat. "I spoke with Marshall last night. I got a phone call yesterday afternoon from a couple of guys I've been talking to."

"Yes?"

"This is going to be my last day," he said.

This was something I had anticipated. "Is that so," I said without any hint of surprise. "Where are you going?"

"There's a place in Cambridge that wants to hire me."

For a while I said nothing. I was now the only servant left on the estate. Marshall was going to die soon. The loneliness I felt suddenly became ten times more intense.

"Well, congratulations. I'm happy for you," I said quietly.

"There's just not going to be anything for us, after Marshall goes. Remember what I told you earlier, Louis. Think about it very carefully."

"I have. I've been thinking of it an awful lot."

"I really hope you find somewhere to go after this. It was an honor working with you."

"Yes. It was an honor working with you, Albert."

We regarded each other for another moment. Then, coldly and yet professionally, I stepped out.

We never saw each other again after that morning. In retrospect now, it was perhaps for the

—dead they're all fucking—

best that he left when he did. Lucky him.

The lounge seemed to close in on me with every minute I waited in it. Alessa often flocked to the lounge throughout the day to write in her notebook or sit before the fire. I stood in a corner, observing the piano and the beautiful Christmas tree. I looked at the fireplace and the old double barrel shotgun hanging over it. Marshall used to go hunting with that shotgun in his younger years but hadn't touched it in at least two decades. The gun cabinet stood directly next to the fireplace, collecting dust.

The door eventually opened and Alessa came in with her notebook tucked under her arm. My intestines knotted inside me. She hadn't noticed my presence, and she approached the sofa and got comfortable on it. I stepped forward and licked my lips. "Alessa," I whispered.

Alessa nearly leapt out of her skin, and she turned around and saw me. "Louis?"

A shy smile came across my face—a defense mechanism to ease the strangeness of my presence. "Sorry. I hope I'm not interrupting anything."

"No, I guess not. Did you want to talk?"

"I did, in fact. I've been thinking a lot since the last time we spoke. I'm a little concerned."

"About what?"

"Your music. You haven't been playing it at night like you said you would."

Alessa looked away. "Oh. I'm sorry. I didn't play."

"Why not? Aren't you still passionate about it?"

"I am, but… it's just, when I play late at night, I thought I was alone. I thought nobody could hear me. I get insecure when I know someone is listening to me play. I'm okay when they hear me do Chopin or something like that, but my own music—it's personal to me. I thought I was the only one who could hear it."

A long silence came between us.

"Please don't be mad, Louis."

"No, it's all right. There was another thing I wanted to speak with you about." With a deep breath I began what I had rehearsed considerably the night before. "You remind me of somebody, Alessa."

"Really? Who?"

"Do you remember when I told you about my sister Josephine? My Sophie."

"Yes?"

I dug out my photograph of Sophie and handed it to her. Alessa took it and considered the photo. "This is her?" she asked.

"Indeed. That is my Sophie. Don't you think that you look a lot like her, Alessa?"

"I mean, I guess. We sorta have the same eyes and nose, but our chins and hair are different. I don't think I look like her."

My face burned. This was not the answer I had been anticipating. As gently as I could, I took the photograph from her. "I think you look very much like her," I said, continuing what I had rehearsed despite the scene not going as planned.

"Tell me, does this photograph fill you with something? Certain sensations? Memories?"

"What are you talking about?"

"Do you remember a frozen lake and a white owl? Ice skating with a young boy?"

"Louis, you're really weirding me out." Fear appeared in her eyes—a deep and uncertain fear. "Why are you asking me all this?"

None of this was supposed to happen—no, she wasn't supposed to react like that! I panicked and tried to put together a convincing sentence that would pull me out of the hole I had dug myself into.

Alessa scurried out of the room and slammed the door shut behind her. I stood, frozen like some statue, humiliated and rejected. All sorts of terrible scenarios played in my head—she was going to tell Henry and Frannie about what just happened, and the whole Turner family—perhaps even Marshall too— would regard me as some sort of freak. Marshall, my best friend, would die feeling ashamed of me.

I left the study and retreated to my quarters downstairs. My greatest fear at that moment was to look at the Turners and have my shame validated by the way they would look at me.

I just wanted *die yes i should have died then and there they would still be alive if* to be with you again Sophie.

There was no way I could leave my room for the rest of that day. Everyone would think me some queer pervert or crazy person. I felt like I had to leave, but where would I go? Who would take in a withering old man?

Again, I considered suicide. It seemed like the only answer, to die in shame, yet I just couldn't. God, how pathetic! *You are pathetic.* Not only was I scared of it, but what would it do to Marshall? I couldn't do such a thing on the eve of his death.

I was trapped. I wanted to scream but all I could do was grit my teeth and quietly suffer. How I wished Alessa would play her music that night.

The whole house was slumbering when I decided to leave my quarters. I went upstairs to the lounge, passing all the golden and silver bells and red and green Christmas lights strung about in the corridor on the way there. Beams of pale moonlight came in through the tall windows, resting against on the piano. I sat before the piano and absently pressed random notes. One note would ring until it fell silent, and then I would press another.

It felt as if centuries had passed since I wept as long and as hard as I did just then—perhaps not since Sophie's death had I cried so severely. I just wanted to be with my sister again before I died. I wanted to tell her how sorry I was for what happened to her, and to receive her forgiveness. The idea of leaving this life without such forgiveness was too horrible to even consider.

The doorknob turned. My weeping ceased and I saw the short figure of Alessa standing in the doorway, hand on the knob, looking at me.

"Louis, are you okay? I heard you crying."

I stood. "I'm sorry. I must have woke you."

"No, I was already awake." She walked up to me. "I couldn't sleep."

Seeing her come so willingly, as if what had transpired the afternoon before meant nothing, made me succumb to my emotions. My worst fears vanished. She accepted me. I got through to her. This was it.

"I was so afraid to show my face to you again," I told her. "Can't you see what I see?"

"Listen Louis, I didn't tell anyone about what happened yesterday. I think you're really hurt by my grandpa dying. I know you and him were friends for a long time. You and my dad should talk. He says you've been acting not yourself and he's worried about you."

Once again, my hopes were crushed. That rage returned, and I no longer had the will to repress it anymore. Everything in my eyes turned red.

"Enough," I firmly said.

"Huh?"

"I said enough! I have been trying to get you to understand, Sophie! I wasn't sure at first, but now I'm convinced. You've done nothing but reject it!"

"What are you talking about, Louis?"

"Can't you see it? You know who you are, Sophie. I know you remember me."

She backed away. "Louis, you're scaring me."

"Please Sophie, don't leave me!" I lunged forward, took her by the arms and pulled her to me. "Please!"

"Louis!" She started to hit me, tried to yank herself out of my grip. "Let go of me! Let go! Stop!"

"I miss you so much, Sophie."

I kissed her on the mouth. She started to scream.

"No!" I shouted. "No, you'll w̄ake them!"

I don't know how it happened. I just remember being absolutely swept by terror. There was no way for me not to be. I threw her to the floor and straddled myself over her and forced my hands over her face, trying to silence her screams.

"Shut up! You'll ruin us!"

Those screams tried to force themselves through my hands, but I just pressed myself down on her harder. Her eyes bulged and pleaded at me to stop. Consumed by terror, I had no idea just how much strength I was using to shut her up. All I know is that at some point in my struggle, I heard a distinctive popping sound, and she stopped screaming. At once what happened became abundantly clear to me.

Sophie stopped moving. Her head limped to one side when I took my hands off her. That still blank face was shaded in the light coming in from the corridor.

"Sophie?"

I fell to my knees and tried to feel for a pulse. There was nothing. Bruises covered her face, neck and shoulders. Good God, what did I do? There was no way I could have used so much strength, was there? On my Maman's grave, I swear I had no idea what I was doing—I didn't want to hurt her! Henry and Frannie were going to wake up and I just needed her to shut up!

"No," I whispered.

Alarm overtook me, burning through my body as if the blood in my veins were kerosene and my heart was the igniting point. Nobody could know what I did; it was an act done purely out of instinct.

I took Sophie into my arms and fled to my quarters downstairs, squeezing her against my chest as if I could somehow will life back into her. My closet was the first thing I saw, and I lay her down inside of it and hid her under several spare sheets and closed the door. A ringing in my ears arose and I swear

please papa dont beat me

im sorry i love you

??????????????

No, I swear to God I had no idea. I love my sister. I didn't mean to hurt her! I was desperate and scared! But *was my only chance to no i cant it cant be like this i have to find* and how can I fix this? It's already too late—I have nowhere to go, I can't do anything *you can always kill yourself* no I can't, I'm too scared *you have to its all you have left you always knew it was going to end* but it cant end like this no i cant *papa should have killed you the moment you murdered sophie* oh please, maman and papa, im so sorry i shouldnt have. Alessasophie i jusT wANted us to be tOGEtHer again. SoPHIEALessA can yU forgive ME?

No… I need to wait. I can figure this out. I can fix this. I just have to give myself a little *if that's what you truly believe…*

Yes. Sophessa, we'll be together. Promise. *Prmise? ido ill doanything.*

In the morning I continued my routine as if it were any other. While I was in the dining room changing a lightbulb, Henry poked his head in and asked: "Del, have you seen Alessa at all this morning?"

"No, Henry. Have you checked the lounge? She spends an awful lot of time in there."

"I've looked everywhere." His voice was shaking. "She wasn't in her bed this morning, either. We always wake up before her. She's not anywhere. Frannie's outside looking for her right now."

I feigned concern. "Really? That's frightening to hear. She has no reason to go anywhere off estate grounds."

"Would you keep an eye out for her please?"

"Absolutely, monsieur."

The front door was heard opening, followed by Frannie's panicked voice calling out for Alessa in the foyer. I rushed in and saw her. Her eyes were wild and her teeth were gnashed. As soon as she saw me, she rushed up to me. "Del! Have you seen Alessa anywhere?"

"I haven't seen her. Henry already told me."

Footsteps stomped across the house and Henry stepped in and went to his wife. "Did you find her?"

"No! She's not anywhere!"

Frannie started to cry and Henry held her face to his chest. I stood afar, watching. Sophie was dead in my closet. There was absolutely no way this was going to end reasonably. Seeing the Turners like this—it just drove the reality of everything straight home for me just then.

"Alessa, my baby," Frannie sobbed. "Where is she, Henry?"

"I don't know. What should we do?"

"Call the police!"

"I don't—I don't know the jurisdiction here. Is Leighton still constable here, Louis?"

"I will call him right away, monsieur," I said.

Just as I was about to step out, Henry's voice halted me.

"Wait, Del."

I turned and saw them staring at me with pleading eyes.

"You won't tell Marshall, will you?" Henry said.

"No, monsieur. I won't."

"Okay." Henry's eyes were glassy and red. "I don't know what the stress of all this will do to him."

"We will find mademoiselle Alessa. I promise you."

"Thank you, Del."

I went to the phone in the kitchen and dialed the constable.

Clarke's Purchase is one of several grants and townships in the White Mountains that isn't part of any town or city metropolitan area and has limited self-government. As such, it has no police force, but has had a constable for some years now named Leighton Hargrave.

Leigh is a seasoned constable who has dealt with all sorts of cases in and around the Purchase, from the Fournier murder-suicide to the awful business that goes on in the Adrienne Forest. He's professional, but also wise and empathetic. Leigh has known me and Marshall for a long time. He knows everyone in the Purchase and is close with the state police too.

When Leigh picked up and I told him that I had a missing persons to report, he took it personally. "Really, Del? Is everything with Marsh all right?"

"No," I said. "His granddaughter has gone missing."

"Well shit, Delacroix. That's just awful. How long she been missing?"

I clicked my tongue, trying to think of an answer. "Since her parents woke up. She wasn't in bed and she's nowhere to be found on the estate or outside."

"Say no more. I'm on my way."

Twenty minutes later Leigh's cruiser passed through the estate front gates. The Turners and I stepped outside to meet him, and he clambered out of his vehicle wearing his fur-collared leather coat and a thumb hooked in his belt strap. "Afternoon, Del. Frannie, Henry—it's been some time since I seen you two."

"It has. Thank you for coming, Leigh," Frannie said

"Del told me your little girl has gone missing and I sped over as fast as I could." He took a notepad from his breast pocket and pulled a pen out of the steel spiral. "Let me hear what all three of you got to say, from the last time you saw, uh—what's her name again?"

"Alessa," Frannie said, with some offense.

Leigh nodded and pressed the tip of his pen to the pad. "The last time you saw Alessa, from the moment you woke up to now. Henry, you start us out, would you?"

One at a time he took our testimonies. When finished, he tucked the notepad back into his pocket. "I tell you what—I'll call the state police at their barracks in Berlin. They'll put together a search party, watching the interstate and going through the forestry. They may want to come over and speak with you as well. I'll call you later tonight or tomorrow morning and check up on things. I'm sorry about all this. We'll find her."

"Thank you, Constable Hargrave," Frannie said. "She's everything to us."

Those last four words dug into my heart like a dagger.

There was no way I could hide what I had done, especially when the state troopers come to the estate. Soon, the stench of rot was going to become obvious in my quarters. I had to get rid of the body, but how? There was no place to conceal it outside—the ground is frozen and the state police would surely comb over every inch of land around the property. There was nowhere in the house I could think of to put her either.

The only thing I could think to do was to take a saw and—

No, I can't even imagine it now. What could I do, Sophie? Je suis vraiment désolé! I cannot say it enough! You gave me a second chance and I ruined it. Il n'ya pas d'espoir.

After Hargrave left, Frannie and Henry retreated to the living room. They laid down on the couch, holding each other with the television on, neither really paying attention to it. I asked them if there was anything I could do for them.

"Just leave us be," Henry said, his voice faint. "Please."

I returned to my quarters. The aroma of feces and urine reeked from the closet. Sophie's body expelled waste as decomposition set in. When I felt strong enough, I opened the closet and focused on that still shape beneath my bedsheets on the floor. Part of me wanted to pull those sheets off and look at her face, but the thought distressed me and I shut the door.

There was one option left to me—there *is* one option left to me. I had finally reached that dead end I so dreaded. The fear of drowning was greater than the fear of what lurks beyond the surface. That night I decided to write out a note explaining everything and begging forgiveness.

First, I needed to say goodbye.

By that point it became too much of an agonizing burden to move Marshall from his bed anymore. Everything, he told me, was uncomfortable, and he wished that it all could just be over with already. He lost his eyesight by that afternoon and even talking was taxing on his energy.

The sound of the oxygen tank feeding Marshall life was heard through his bedroom door. When I stepped in, I gazed at my poor wasted friend. He looked centuries old.

"Del, is that you?" he asked the room.

"Yes, monsieur."

"Come here for a second."

I stood at his bedside with my hands neatly pressed in front of me. "I'm here."

"How are you doing, Del?" His glassy eyes searched for me. "I can't see you. I can't see anything. Everything is just black."

"I know, monsieur," I said, swallowing my emotion as best as I could. "I'm fine—as fine as I can be, I think."

"Where's my family, Del?"

I had anticipated this question and already had a preemptive answer ready, but it still unsettled me to hear it asked. "They're downstairs. Alessa is being tutored now, but perhaps I can send for them later."

Marshall waved his hand. "I'd like to have a moment alone with you anyways."

"Monsieur?"

"Being here in bed for so long—so close to going out—it's got me thinking. Del, did you lead a happy life?"

The question confused me. "Pardon?"

"I know where you came from, Del. I know how your parents treated you. When I first saw you all those years ago, you looked like some scared, abused little dog." He chuckled, then coughed. "But I saw the work you did. I knew you had a will of iron. I hadn't had Henry yet and I saw so much in you. I says to myself, 'This kid, he's a little wet behind the ears, but I bet I can straighten him out into something respectable.'"

My throat tightened, and I tried not to let Marshall hear me cry. "Yes, I remember," I said.

Marshall turned his head to me. His eyes were like milky jewels; without color or life. "Did I give you a happy life?"

"Yes, Marshall. I can't imagine how my life would have turned out had I not met you."

"I'm glad." He turned his head away and closed those terrible eyes. "You were always good to me. Starting your own business, you meet a lot of people that wanna make you to think they're your pals, you know? But really they're just trying to get something out of you. You weren't like that, Del."

"Thank you, monsieur."

"Henry, my only kid… I did as well as I could with him, but sometimes I feel like I was just training him to take my place when the time came." He paused, struggled to resume. "I wish I had played ball with him a little more when he was a kid, instead of making him learn spreadsheets. You were a better dad to him than me, Del."

I couldn't think of anything to say to this. I pressed my hand to my mouth, unable to contain the grief.

"The point is," Marshall went on, "is that you are my best friend. You are my only friend. The only loyal person I've ever had. Take good care of Alessa, would you? Make sure she's happy. I know Henry is raising her rough and straight like how I raised him. Play ball with her now and then, would you?"

As cruel as it may sound, I was comforted by the fact that Marshall couldn't see me in that moment. I must have resembled a shattering mirror. "Yes, monsieur," I said, wiping my face.

"Thank you, Del. Loyal to the end. So long as Alessa is happy, I'll go out happy."

I leaned in and kissed Marshall on the temple. His morose face glowed dimly.

"I'm tired, old friend," he said. "Let me go to sleep, wouldya?"

Somberly, I left the room. Before I shut the door, I peeked at him as he lay motionless on his deathbed. "Au revoir, vieil ami," I whispered.

That was the last time I saw my friend alive.

Night consumed the estate. Frannie and Henry departed to their guestroom and locked the door. When I knew I was alone, I took a bottle of champagne from the kitchen and sleeping pills from the bathroom, then crept into my quarters downstairs.

Upon the doorknob of the closet I tied one end of a leather belt. The plan was to down the pills with champagne and then hang myself. There was no way I would survive. The horror of it tried to prevent me from doing it, but the reality of my situation demanded it. There was no going back from what I had done. This was the only logical step I had left.

The photo of Sophie sat on my desk, watching me as I wrote my suicide note. I would get three paragraphs in before tearing it to shreds and beginning anew. There was so much I had to confess, but none of it was coming out in the way it needed to. I drank the champagne as I worked, hoping it would make things easier. With every dissatisfied rejection of one letter and the start of another, I drank a glass. My thoughts became hazy and my hands went numb. The words on the paper started to swim in my eyes.

I don't know what time it was, but it was late in the night when I heard it. I thought I was just imagining things. I set my pen aside and listened closely. It was the piano upstairs. Somebody was playing on it.

The sound of its strings ringing out notes were quiet at first, then became louder until I could finally make out what it was. I couldn't believe it. I stood from my desk, staring up at the ceiling, listening.

It was Alessa's melody—the one she played the night we first spoke alone in the lounge. Except it was awful. Good Lord it was the most terrible thing I ever heard. The notes were so off-key and aggressively played that it felt like icepicks piercing my ears. My hands came up to the sides of my head and I tried to block out the noise.

"Who are you—why are you doing this?" I drunkenly shouted.

I staggered out of my quarters and went upstairs. I needed to see who was playing the piano and ruining Alessa's beautiful music to torture me. Once down the corridor I threw open the lounge door and stepped in. The horrible music became deafening now; my skull was pounding.

Within the moonlight creeping through the windows I could see the piano. The ivory keys were pressing down by themselves. Crimson red fluid bled from between the keys and pooled into dark splotches on the carpet.

"Stop it!" I screamed. "For the love of God, shut the fuck up!"

It did not cease. The playing just got worse, more aggressive, louder. It was punishing me.

"Please stop! You're killing me! S'il vous plait! Arrêtez!"

On the mantle of the fireplace I saw an iron poker. I grasped it and began smashing the piano keys to make it stop. The keys splintered and cracked, and pieces of them flew all around the room, but the music did not stop. Blood poured like a spring from the smashed keys, and the sounds the instrument made became only more deranged and appalling than before.

I grasped the poker in both hands and backed into a corner. "I'm sorry," I cried. "Please, I'm sorry. Je suis désolé. Please, just STOP!"

That was when I saw her. Transparent in the moonlight, sitting at the piano, was Sophie. Her body was decomposed, and her gray skin was pulled tightly over her bones. Maggots poured from her mouth and eye sockets as her fingers orchestrated the bloody keys of the piano.

"Sophie, I'm sorry! My baby sister! Forgive me, please! I didn't mean to kill you!"

"Del!"

Henry stood in the doorway, horrified by me—horrified by Sophie playing the piano.

That was it. After all these years, I'm found out. Sophie was playing her music to tell the Turners that I murdered her—

forcing me to confess! They couldn't *ill never survive in prison* know *i didn't wanT to Do it ihaDto kiLl them i had no chice* THEY COULDN'T KNOW.

I dove across the room with the poker and bludgeoned Henry. The poker grazed his face, the horn tearing his cheek apart, and he fell to the floor. His hands rose *fucker needed to die* over his head.

"Del, what are you doing? Stop!"

The disfigured music pounded in my ears, tearing my mind apart. I brought the poker down on Henry repeatedly until his face looked like raw beef. My frail old body exhausted itself, so I took the double barrel shotgun from over the fireplace and *just like how papa showed me* loaded two shells from the cabinet into

!!!—je suis si désolé maman et papa s'il vous plaît ne me faites pas de mal J'ai adoré Sophie—!!!

and returned to the doorway. Henry was trying to crawl away. I shot one barrel into his spine and he went flat against the floor, then I shot the other barrel into the back of his head. Shards of skull bone and pink bits of brain *like confetti, during sophies birthday* splattered the floor and my clothes.

I returned to the cabinet, reloaded the shotgun, then made my way to the guest bedroom.

Frannie Turner stood outside the guest bedroom in her white nightgown, alerted to the shots. The moment she saw me come around the corner, she shrieked *maman i love you* and ran back into the room. I chased after her, and she fled into the bathroom, but before she could shut the door, I shot her and she fell backwards into the bathtub.

With one barrel of the shotgun smoking, I stepped in and watched as she struggled to pull herself out of the tub with one hand and tried to keep her intestines from spilling out with the other *such colorful organs.*

Through the piano's deranged music booming in my head, I heard her beg, "Why are you doing this?"

I sobbed and the shotgun trembled in my grip. I told her that I was sorry, then thumbed back on the hammer, pulled the trigger on the second barrel and shot her in the face.

The gun dropped from my hands to the floor. I stood marveling at the ruined mess that had once been Francine Turner. The sensation of warm, irony blood in my clothes and on my skin was finally sensed. I could taste that blood on my lips.

The wind blew against the windows, whistling. The melody *sweet sweet silence* had ceased. My ears rung in the sudden quiet after all the violence ended. I was all alone.

Alessa's Melody

It's Christmas Eve now.

Sometime before or after I had done away with the Turners, Marshall passed away. I went upstairs to my old friend's bedroom and found that he was gone.

I sat by his side, admiring his beautiful face. He was smiling, having left this world content. It made me feel good to see him like this. I felt content as well, because I finally understood what I needed to do. I kissed him, covered him with his blanket, then went outside to the shed to grab a container of gasoline.

You see, I was never meant to live on. That is why she came back—I was supposed to die that day all those years ago in 1960. Sophie and I were supposed to drown together in that frozen lake. She hadn't come back to me after fifty-seven years so that I could somehow redeem myself—it was so that we could finally die together, as one. As brother and sister united.

Surely the state police and perhaps even Constable Hargrave will come soon, so I must work quickly. I wrapped Frannie and Henry up in tablecloths and put them in the kitchen storeroom, then took Sophie out of my closet and lay her on my bed. I've just finished pouring gasoline all over the house, and I have a candle burning away near where most of it is soaked in Marshall's bedroom.

Sophie is in my arms now, and I can smell smoke and feel the heat of the fire on the second floor. I pull Sophie into my chest, kissing her, loving her. Oh Sophie. How I missed you. I no longer fear death because I'm no longer alone. We'll leave this world together, consummated in flame, and cross to the other side as one.

We are a force that shouldn't ever have been separated. I'm sorry it took me so long to set this right. I love you, Josephine. My heart and soul, I give my life to you.

Je te donne ma vie.

Sophie…

—it burns—

2017

Jayson Robert Ducharme

Alessa's Melody

Thank you for purchasing *Alessa's Melody*.

If you enjoyed this book, please consider leaving a review on Amazon. Every review helps the book's ranking and visibility. If you'd like updates on future content, free promotions, giveaways, and more, then subscribe to my newsletter at www.jaysonrobertducharme.com.

J.R.D.

Printed in Great Britain
by Amazon

75965863R00054